Amazing Grace

For Thida Aye Stirrup with love - may all your dreams come true
(apart from the very silly ones, obviously) — M.H.

For Kanju — C.B.

Text copyright © Mary Hoffman 1991
Illustrations copyright © Caroline Binch 1991

The rights of Mary Hoffman and Caroline Binch to be identified as the Author
and Illustrator of this Work have been asserted by them in accordance
with the Copyright, Designs and Patents Act, 1988 (United Kingdom).
First published in Great Britain in 1991 by
Frances Lincoln Children's Books,
74-77 White Lion Street, London, N1 9PF
www.franceslincoln.com

This hardback edition first published in Great Britain in 2015

British Library Cataloguing in Publication Data available on request

ISBN 978-1-84780-593-5

Printed in China

1 3 5 7 9 8 6 4 2

Amazing Grace

Mary Hoffman

Illustrated by Caroline Binch

Frances Lincoln
Children's Books

How it all began... by Mary Hoffman and Caroline Binch

"Once there was a little girl who loved stories…"

As I wrote that in 1989, I had just been for a swim, and was far away from phone calls or rings at the doorbell or the demands of my three daughters aged from seven to twelve. I had no idea this would lead to seven books and many spin-offs. It was one of the most momentous beginnings ever but of course I didn't know it.

In 2016 *Amazing Grace* will be twenty-five years old! And yet Grace herself remains, with her gappy smile, somewhere around six or seven. At her age I loved stories best of everything – and I still do! I have made my career writing them, but long before that happened I was to stories as a vacuum-cleaner is to dust.

And, like Grace, as soon as I had heard them, I wanted to act them out. My long-suffering family, particularly my sister Phyllis, had to take all the other parts while I starred as Cinderella or Aladdin or Beauty.

One thing was different: I had no grandmother. (And no grandfather either.) I made up for this misfortune by "collecting" older people throughout my childhood. Now I am a grandmother myself and can't wait to tell stories to my grandbabies.

If *Amazing Grace* has a message – which I am often asked about – it is that all stories are for all people. I believe this from the bottom of my heart. May you find the right stories for you and then please pass them on. The more stories everyone knows the more likely they are to be kinder, friendlier and more accepting of others.

That's the amazing thing about stories.

Mary M Hoffman

Amazing Grace arrived in my letterbox 26 years ago as a couple of sheets of printed paper.

Mary Hoffman had admired the cover artwork I had done for her book, *Ip Dip Sky Blue* – a collection of stories – and had asked the publishers if I could be the illustrator for her new story.

Reading *Amazing Grace* for the first time, I felt a tingle of excitement. Yes! I would love to visualise this terrific character and her world.

I paint realistic images from photographs that I take, so the first step was to find the people to play the parts. My aim is always that the illustrations also tell the story by facial expressions and body language, alongside the text. Because of this I felt it was important to find a real life Nana, Ma and daughter.

Ibrahim, my Nigerian friend, knew of such a family, whom I subsequently met and arranged to take photos of; my part in the creation of *Amazing Grace* had begun.

What a joy it was to give a visual interpretation of this lively and determined character as she acted, imagined and danced her way into so many hearts; inspiring children all over the world for so many years.

Caroline Binch

Grace was a girl who loved stories.

She didn't mind if they were read to her or told to her or made up in her own head. She didn't care if they were from books or on TV or in films or on the video or out of Nana's long memory. Grace just loved stories.

And after she had heard them, or sometimes while they were still going on, Grace would act them out. And she always gave herself the most exciting part.

Grace went into battle as Joan of Arc...

and wove a wicked web as Anansi the spiderman.

She hid inside the wooden horse at the gates of Troy...

She crossed the Alps with Hannibal and a hundred elephants...

She sailed the seven seas
with a peg-leg
and a parrot.

She was Hiawatha, sitting by the shining Big-Sea-Water

and Mowgli in the back garden jungle.

But most of all Grace loved to act pantomimes. She liked to
be Dick Whittington turning to hear the bells of London Town
or Aladdin rubbing the magic lamp. The best characters in
pantomimes were boys, but Grace played them anyway.

When there was no one else around, Grace played all the parts
herself. She was a cast of thousands. Paw-Paw the cat usually
helped out.

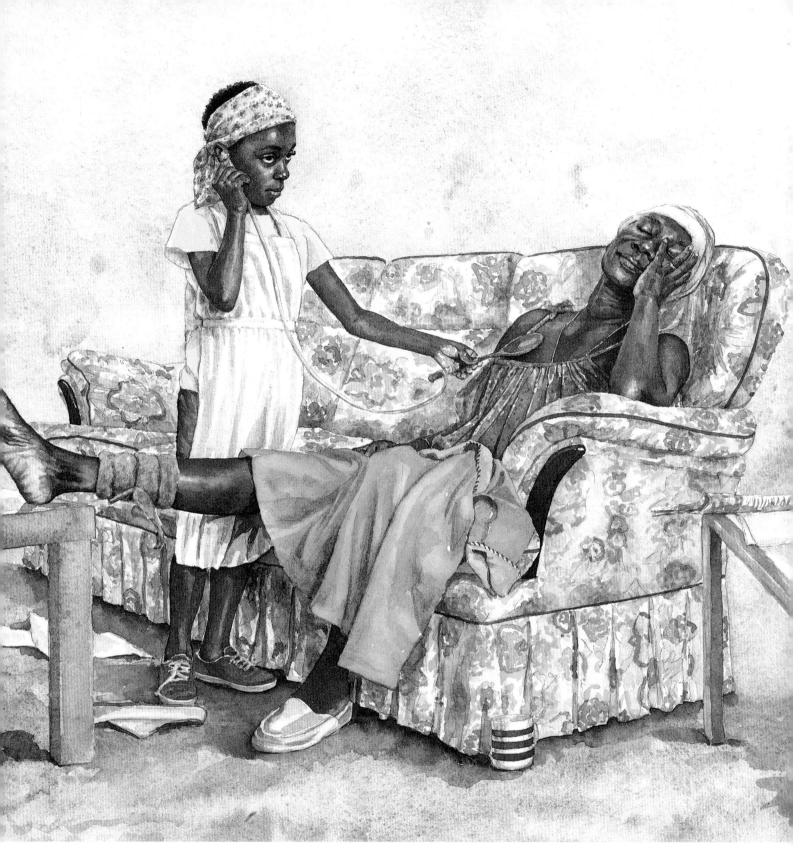

And sometimes she could persuade Ma and Nana to join in,
when they weren't too busy. Then she was Doctor Grace and
their lives were in her hands.

One day at school her teacher said they were going to do the play of *Peter Pan*. Grace put up her hand to be… Peter Pan.

"You can't be called Peter," said Raj. "That's a boy's name."

But Grace kept her hand up.

"You can't be Peter Pan," whispered Natalie.
"He wasn't black." But Grace kept her hand up.

"All right," said the teacher. "Lots of you want to be
Peter Pan, so we'll have to have auditions.
We'll choose the parts next Monday."

When Grace got home, she seemed rather sad.

"What's the matter?" asked Ma.

"Raj said I couldn't be Peter Pan because I'm a girl."

"That just shows all Raj knows about it," said Ma. "Peter Pan is *always* a girl!"

Grace cheered up, then later she remembered something else.
"Natalie says I can't be Peter Pan because I'm black," she said.

Ma started to get angry but Nana stopped her.

"It seems that Natalie is another one who don't know nothing," she said. "You can be anything you want, Grace, if you put your mind to it."

Next day was Saturday and Nana told Grace they were going out. In the afternoon they caught a bus and a train into town. Nana took Grace to a grand theatre. Outside it said, "ROSALIE WILKINS in ROMEO AND JULIET" in beautiful sparkling lights.

"Are we going to the ballet, Nana?" asked Grace.

"We are, Honey, but I want you to look at these pictures first."

Nana showed Grace some photographs of a beautiful young girl dancer in a tutu. "STUNNING NEW JULIET!" it said on one of them.

"That one is little Rosalie from back home in Trinidad," said Nana. "Her granny and me, we grew up together on the island. She's always asking me do I want tickets to see her little girl dance — so this time I said yes."

After the ballet, Grace played the part of Juliet, dancing around her room in her imaginary tutu.

"I can be anything I want," she thought. "I can even be Peter Pan."

On Monday they had the auditions. Their teacher let the class vote on the parts. Raj was chosen to play Captain Hook. Natalie was going to be Wendy.

Then they had to choose Peter Pan.

Grace knew exactly what to do – and all the words to say. It was a part she had often played at home. All the children voted for her.

The play was a great success and Grace was an amazing
Peter Pan.

After it was all over, she said, "I feel as if I could fly
all the way home!"

"You probably could," said Ma.

"Yes," said Nana. "If Grace put her mind to it —
she can do anything she want."

Happy 25th Birthday to *Amazing Grace* – from Floella Benjamin

As soon as I saw Caroline Binch's superb picture on the cover of *Amazing Grace*, I knew this was the book all children, especially those from diverse backgrounds, had been waiting for.

During my time presenting children's TV programmes and telling picture book stories, I became fully aware of just what a vibrant, varied range of kids there were in this country. But when I came to judge a prize for children's books in the 1980s, it was shamefully apparent that this wasn't reflected in the words and pictures I saw being produced for children and their families.

Then, nearly twenty-five years ago, along came Grace, the girl who learned from stories, as well as from the warm support of her mother and grandmother. A little girl I recognised because I had been like her myself.

"At last!" I thought. "A book about the thousands of children who all longed to see themselves reflected in stories."

It wasn't any use telling Grace she couldn't do something just because she was a girl or because she was black. It was saying 'yes you can if you try hard and are good enough'. Grace kept her hand up. And of course she was picked to play Peter Pan because she was the best person for the part.

It's a message that we still need 25 years on – that we can be and do anything we want if we just put our minds to it. Nana never said a wiser word.

So, keep on enjoying stories like Grace and, most of all, believe in yourselves and you will soon be flying, just like Peter Pan.

Floella Benjamin

Baroness Floella Benjamin, OBE

In celebration of *Amazing Grace* – by LeVar Burton

Amazing Grace is one of my favourite children's books of all time. Whenever I am asked for a recommendation for an exceptional picture book, "Grace" is always at the top of my list. In Grace's struggle for acceptance of who she is, I see myself: a person fiercely determined to obliterate the bonds of lack and limitation that continue to afflict citizens of colour in this world.

Growing up in the midst of the Civil Rights Movement in America, I, like Grace, benefitted from the wise council and costly sacrifices made by those who came before me. My mother, the first in our family to graduate from college, consistently reminded me that as I grew up, I would inherit a world that would oftentimes be hostile to my presence, simply because of the colour of my skin. Her untold sacrifices, and those of her generation, were calculated to provide opportunities and advantages that they themselves never enjoyed. And this paved the way for me and my generation to achieve a semblance of equality in a society dominated by Euro-centric systems of behaviour and belief, founded on the legacy of slavery and institutional racism.

It is not insignificant to note that the kind of universal wisdom that can only be forged in the fires of oppression followed by forgiveness, are on full display in Mary Hoffman's depiction of Grace's journey. In her portrait of this child, delivered from the Afro-Caribbean diaspora to the melting pot of New York City or London, Mary elegantly and eloquently communicates the pain of prejudice as well as the soaring triumph of the human spirit, spurred by the enduring belief that all humans are created equally.

Alex Haley, the author of *Roots*, used to say, "Find the good and praise it!" In recommending *Amazing Grace* to audiences of today, I am content in the knowledge that his admonition is alive and well.

LeVar Burton